UNREMEMBERED HISTORIES
SIX STORIES WITH A SUPERNATURAL TWIST

ED NEWMAN

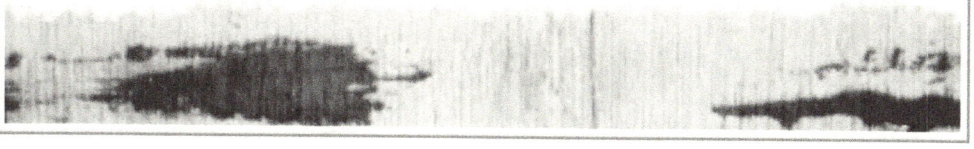

Dedication 5

Unremembered Histories 7

Preface 8

Two Acts That 10

Changed the World 10

The Empty Space 18

Duel of the Poets 26

Unrecorded Histories 38

The Nonsense Room 60

Acknowledgements 73

Dedication

To all lovers of short fiction and to the writers who preceded us with the stories that so shaped our lives.

Unremembered Histories

Six Stories with a Supernatural Twist

Copyright 2011 Ed Newman

All rights reserved

ISBN 978-1490460086

N&L Publishing

No part of this book may be reproduced in any manner without the express written consent of the publisher except in the case of brief excerpts in reviews, articles, or blogs discussing the book. All inquires should be addressed to PublishingNL@gmail.com.

N&L Publishing books may be purchased in bulk for sales promotions, corporate gifts, fund-raising, or for educational purposes.

N&L Publishing

Ed Newman & TJ Lind

www.ennyman.com

Preface

In the first part of the 20th century, when the short story form was in its prime, F. Scott Fitzgerald sometimes received three times more for a single story than the average American earned in a year. A good storyteller had real value in our culture. In the days before movie theaters and television, magazines like The Saturday Evening Post offered some of the best entertainment around. And they paid well to get those marquis writers on their covers.

Even though times have changed, I'm still a believer in the short story form. In the late 1970's one writer whose stories made a profound impact on me was Ernest Hemingway. Hemingway's *In Our Time* hit me like a fist when I first encountered it. The forcefulness of his prose influenced the whole direction of literature, even if the man himself has gone out of favor in some circles.

The stories in this volume owe a debt to another writer who was himself a master of the short story form, Jorge Luis Borges. The stories here incorporate elements of the paranormal and the supra-natural. "The Nonsense Room" and "Duel of the Poets," which was translated into

Croatian as the centerpiece for a poetry site, were both directly influenced by this Argentine author of what some have called magical realism, though it's my own opinion that his stories defy such easy categorization.

Perhaps one day the same will be said of my own. For now, it's my hope that you will find them entertaining, engaging and thought-provoking... and worth sharing with your very best friends so you can talk about them over a good bottle of wine.

Two Acts That Changed the World

Of the dozen or so German physicists who had been assigned the task of building a super-bomb for Germany, Wilhelm Kurtweil more than any knew the consequences for humanity should the Nazis succeed in being the first to achieve this. Kurtweil had been a leading voice in German physics before the war, was now a respected scientist in the twilight years of a fabulous career.

For him personally, Nazism was an odious blight on the German peoples, but he had remained silent, hoping against hope that the dark season would pass and German character would rise above its brutal cancer. By 1942 he'd lost this hope.

The super-bomb project was in full swing. The Nazis already dominated Europe. England was about to fall. His worst fear of all: that the project succeed and his name forever be associated with its success in bringing the world to its knees at Hitler's feet.

In November he began praying for divine intervention. He did not believe in God, but not knowing where else to turn and hoping that he was wrong, he prayed that God would give him wisdom. The following week he conceived in a dream, visualized with perfect clarity, the formulation for the Atomic Bomb. It was so perfect, so brilliantly conceived, and remarkably clever. He woke in a sweat. With his mind over-stimulated he spent the rest of that night hastily scratching notes on scraps of paper. For three successive nights he worked out the details, occasionally catching fitful moments of sleep to sustain his strength.

On the fourth night, he saw the two actions he must take. First, he must find a way to undermine -- without drawing suspicion -- the efforts of his fellow scientists. And second, he must find a way to communicate his findings to the American scientists whom he believed were actively pursuing the same designs.

The first task was easy enough. He saw clearly that the labyrinthian formula was built on a series of equations that flowed with a counterintuitive divergence from logic at several critical points. How he had seen this so plainly baffled him. In presenting his discoveries to the group, he merely had to re-arrange the equation at two points and the system would forever fail to detonate. Once these two re-arrangements were made, no amount of re- evaluation would point to this particular detail as being faulty. All corrections of the misfire would focus on other areas of the formulation, with over one hundred million permutations. If all went well, it would be ten years before the mistake was discovered.

Though he intended to delay as long as possible the presentation of his formulation, he knew he must be the first to present, lest the correct thesis be presented in regards to the critical path. By early spring of 1943 he saw that two of his young protégés were uncovering significant portions of the path and he was forced to the first task. On April seventh, he presented his findings with cool reserve and astounding humility. The team was ecstatic at the breakthrough.

The second task proved more daunting. He must find a way to communicate his findings to a team of American scientists that would be assembling in pursuit of the same objective. It was well-known by Nazi intelligence who America's leading scientists were. There were well placed Germans among them. He must secretly make contact and pass along his findings. So great was his fear of creating suspicions that he never once dared to speak to anyone of his intentions.

In June a secret memo crossed his desk requesting him to cease from all projects not related to the superbomb. An attachment for his eyes only mentioned that it was now going to be a race. The Americans were indeed assembling their own team, and time was not an ally.

Near the end of the attachment he noted a list of names, the names of prominent scientists with whom the German team was in direct competition. Among the names was a certain Robert Oppenheimer and it seemed as if the letters of his name leaped from the page and were branded into his consciousness.

"Oppenheimer," he said to himself.

"Did you say something, Herr Kurtweil?" one of his associates asked.

Kurtweil did not reply. Inwardly he vowed to make contact with Oppenheimer.

By late summer he realized that normal communication channels were closed to him. There was no way he would risk divulging his secrets, for there was no one he trusted. Yes, he knew there were malcontents among the ranks, but the magnitude of the stakes made it impossible for him to risk having such knowledge fall into the wrong hands, that is, Nazi hands.

According to a notation in his journals, on September 12, unable to find sleep, Kurtweil rose from his bed and dressed to go out, perhaps to a cabaret, perhaps for a smoke. When he opened the door he was startled to find a strange stooped man standing on his doorstep.

"What do you want?" Kurtweil said sharply.

"I have watched you, Herr Kurtweil. The destiny of the world is in your hands."

"Who are you? Why are you here?"

"I have come to help you. May I come in?"

Kurtweil was frightened. Did someone know? Had something in his manner betrayed him?

The man put his hand on Kurtweil's arm. "I know the solution to your problem."

Kurtweil began to stammer. He had not been sleeping. He had not had enough rest. He tried to pull back, but the stranger held him firmly.

When their eyes met, Kurtweil saw that he was not in danger. "Come in," he said with resignation.

They walked to the back of the house to Kurtweil's study. It was badly lit so that the corners remained well cloaked in shadow, as were the recesses of his soul.

The man removed his overcoat. Kurtweil threw it over the back of a chair and gave him an ashen look when his empty hands fell to his sides.

"You understand my dilemma," Kurtweil said.

"Yes," said the man quietly.

They seated themselves and for a long time neither spoke. "So what must I do?" Kurtweil said.

"You must learn the secret of dreams."

"What do you mean?"

"Dreaming is not a passive encounter with our unconscious, as Freud taught. Jung was more astute. Yet even Jung did not go far enough. I tell you truthfully, the power of the dream exceeds all known powers, and when you have mastered it, you can save the world."

"I don't understand."

"You are a great mind. Have you no imagination? You wish to communicate a great truth to another great mind. You are trapped by circumstance, by geography, by space and time. How is it possible to escape such bounds?"

"If I knew that, I would be..." He broke off. "You would be... what?"

"God."

"Or ...?"

"Or the devil."

"Think again," the man said.

Kurtweil stood up and walked to the window. He saw his face reflected in the glass, illumined as if a mask, his eyes dark hollows. When he turned again, he was alone. The man had disappeared.

From his pocket he pulled a hanky and dabbed at his forehead. He was sweating profusely and felt a need to take in the night air. Had it been a hallucination? He had not been sleeping well. He had not been sleeping at all, it seemed.

He had met Carl Jung once. They stood together on a balcony at a party in Geneva fifteen years before. "Consciousness is a portal," Jung had said that night. "When we pass through this portal to the other side, where do we go? When we return, where have we been?" Kurtweil, a practical man, was irritated by Jung at the time. But now, he wondered.

During a press conference in 1947 when he was appointed head of the Atomic Energy Commission, J. Robert Oppenheimer was asked how he solved the problem of predetonation and discovered the secret of the bomb. "If I told you the truth you would laugh, so I will only say that it came to me in a dream."

"What kind of dream, sir? Did you see blueprints or something like that?"

Oppenheimer hesitated a moment, then replied, "Actually, it was someone else's dream." This cryptic reply is the only known public reference to Dr. Kurtweil's second great achievement.

***

Author's Note: I learned the above story in 1994 while teaching a class for senior citizens at University of MN, Duluth. That spring I'd written a series of articles on ethical issues in terminal health care and as a result had been invited to teach for an afternoon on the pros and cons of assisted suicide. One of the members of the class was a large man whose name now escapes me (I have it written in my notes somewhere, but for the sake of this story I will call him Mr. Jackson) who, as a young scientist, had been a member of the Manhattan Project. Being a writer I am always interested in a good story. I asked if he had plans for dinner.

Mr. Jackson told me that during the course of the project Oppenheimer had become a changed man. "It happened almost suddenly. Most of us attributed it to the fact that we had had a breakthrough and the Bomb was going to become a reality."

I had worked closely with Robert," Jackson continued, "and sensed it to be something more, so we went out one night and I confronted him. He made me swear oaths of silence, then stated coldly that if the truth were made public he would be considered a lunatic and removed from the project. 'I could be ruined,' he said. As we all know the Project was a success and Oppenheimer became a national hero. I've often wondered who else knew the source of his inspiration, or whether I was the only one."

The Empty Space

I heard this story from Stuart M----, caretaker of an apartment complex on Stevens Square in South Minneapolis in the early 80's when I made my living as a painting contractor. After a fire in one of the buildings Dennis, my painting partner, and I spent quite a number of weeks there painting walls, ceilings, stairwells and doors. On the surface the likable and loquacious Stu appears eager to engage in the typical banter one expects from those elaborately involved with a public. I soon perceived that this was all an act and thereafter I determined to respect his privacy.

At the end of a particularly busy week I was washing out paint rollers and brushes in the laundry room when Stu came in. "You got plans for dinner?" he asked. It surprised me, though I appreciated his thoughtfulness. I assumed it was because he was lonely. His wife was out of town. Having no other plans I felt inclined to accept the offer. Dennis had taken off early to go camping with his family.

At some point during the meal Stu told me that his wife had taken a one-year journalism position in St. Louis in order to get newspaper experience. He made contradictory remarks about her absence, saying that it felt good to be alone, and then again saying that he missed her terribly.

Over dinner we shared a bottle of wine, and through the course of the evening a second. It was late when I realized the evening had fled. He asked me not to leave. I reminded him that it was almost midnight and made a lame joke about turning into a pumpkin. He said he had something he needed to talk about.

Evidently he had wanted to be certain about me before he could share what was really on his heart. Perhaps the wine added to his courage. As near as I can reproduce it, this is the story Stuart told that night. To my shame I pretended to believe every word.

Here's Stuart's story:

I owe the discovery of the 'empty space' to the death of my father. Within a week after the funeral I began searching for an apartment in South Minneapolis to be near my ailing mom and came upon an available efficiency just off Hennepin in the Uptown district.

While the manager was showing the room I asked questions. He spoke in short, dramatic bursts in a manner I found unsettling, so I probed more deeply and learned that the apartment had been let to at least four tenants in the previous year. When he asked me to sign a year's lease, I was surprised that four successive tenants would break that kind of a contract. You can tell how badly I wanted the place since I signed the lease anyways. Later I learned that as many as six tenants had occupied the apartment that year.

The efficiency was located in one of those old-fashioned buildings built in the 1890's with exaggerated baseboards, a Murphy bed, and ten layers of wallpaper. While moving in I learned from a woman across the hallway that the room was haunted. When I asked in what way, the lady couldn't explain.

"Is it ghosts? Was someone murdered here?"

She said that wasn't it, but didn't offer any more than that.

My very first night I became aware of it but didn't know what it was. After all the commotion of moving in I put the radio on till late, pulled the bed out of the wall and turned in. It's a downtown apartment complex, so one expects a certain amount of noise. While lying in bed I kept hearing the sound of a breeze blowing, crickets, and the rustling of leaves. What was strange about all this is that the windows were closed. Furthermore, there were no trees alongside the apartment building. The nearest tree was across the square. The noise seemed as if it were right there in the room.

I was too exhausted to investigate the source of the sound and fell off into a deep sleep. The following morning I was awakened by the singing of birds and the loud cawing of a crow. I sat up with alarm, again noting that the windows were closed. The birdsongs came from somewhere within the room. It was as if there were a speaker in the room playing one of those nature recordings. I was confused, walking about from here to there in my small space, unable to see anything, but clearly recognizing that the noises were vividly present. Upon more serious investigation I was able to determine that the sound was most prominent in a region approximately two feet from the ceiling and three feet from the corner furthest from the bed.

Throughout the day I told myself it was not too late to break the contract and find another place, but I demurred. A week passed. Occasionally I heard the lowing of cattle. On other occasions the voice of a woman. Once I heard children playing a game. Several times the distant barking of a dog. Most of the time it was the wind, and a few birds. Early evenings, the cattle. After nightfall, the crickets.

I consulted a friend who believes in all kinds of strange phenomenon. He was an avid sci fi fan and had all those Frank Edwards books like *Stranger Than Science*, things like that. I told him it seemed as if there were a microphone somewhere picking up sounds and projecting them into my room. He found it 'interesting.'

I wouldn't tell my mother about the room. She doesn't like things she can't control or explain. Occasionally I would catch my neighbor across the hall studying me. The old man next door also asked how I felt about the room. I got that fishbowl feeling about my neighbors and it made me want to withdraw.

While doing laundry, a white-haired lady from the third floor said that she heard I had the room with the empty space in it. I asked what an 'empty space' was and she said she didn't know. That's just what she was told it was called.

I consulted with my friend again -- Michael Tucci is his name -- and asked what an 'empty space' is. He said he'd talk to a woman who works at the food co-op. 'She's into all that occult stuff,' he said. 'If it's weird she's into it.'

The following night, he came to my apartment with an older couple who said they once had an empty space behind their house. I don't remember their last names. His name was Ralph, and he called her Flo. "These empty spaces are very rare," the old man said. "You could hear the ocean. It was smashing on the rocks somewhere. Occasionally we'd hear a fishing boat."

"We were living in Iowa, mind you," Flo announced.

"What causes it?" I asked.

"Reality is ever expanding. It's filling more and more space all the time. Mass doesn't expand as fast as reality and so there are cracks or fissures, empty spaces. Noises enter the empty spaces in the same way sound travels through vents in a house." Flo was nodding as Ralph offered his explanation of the phenomenon.

"But how can sound from the country be this loud in my room here in the city? Sound can't travel that far."

"Here, I brought a book that explains that," Ralph said. He had in his hand Volume III of Alexander Manchester's *Tertius Dictum*. "Each point of the universe contains all points... Because there is an infinitely small distance between each point in space, all points in space are immediately present to all other points.... Matter creates the illusion of space and distance.... Empty spaces eliminate this distance." The book went on for several pages in that manner.

Flo told how her life was changed by the presence of the empty space behind their house. "The experience shattered all my preconceived notions about the nature of things. I began to realize things can be different from what we expect. My whole understanding of perceptions and the nature of reality shifted. You might say I began to distrust things other people take for granted."

"In other words," Ralph explained, "she stopped accepting everything she was taught and started thinking for herself."

"It was like an awakening. As if I woke from a deep sleep. I became conscious," Flo explained, "became enthralled by our world. Became, well, infatuated with life."

"Of course, you can go too far, you know," Ralph inserted.

"What do you mean?" I ask.

"I mean, just because some things are different than you expected, not every wacko idea is necessarily true. Take flying saucers, for example. Maybe yes, maybe no. I don't know." My friend Michael frowned because he liked to believe one day he'd see a flying saucer or make contact with aliens.

By evening's end we explored topics as diverse as the Great Pyramids, Atlantis, black holes, werewolves, Ouija, the arcana, witches, black cats and the sephiroth.

To be honest with you, I didn't like these people. They were strange to me. I mean, sure, they told some wild stories like you wouldn't believe, and some you don't want to believe, but it's pretty weird stuff and, for me, when they left that night I was glad to close the door behind them. The good piece in their visit was when we all stopped to listen to a dog howling at one point. It confirmed that I was not a complete lunatic after all.

Then again, where did it leave me? Normal people thought I was the strange one to have this hole in my room that went to the country. And these other people...

A lot of it has to do with the way I grew up. My family was a little different to begin with, and then, too, it seems like we moved every two years so I was always an outsider, always having to prove myself, always the odd man out. You'd think that a kid growing up like that would eventually become skilled at making adjustments, but I never did. Now here I was trying to live a normal life yet I had this bizarre thing going on right in my living space.

The one good thing that happened that night was this. Once I had some kind of explanation for it, I no longer wondered whether I was losing it, if you know what I mean. Up till then I had this knot in my stomach because I harbored a fear that maybe I was cracking up somehow.

You see, when I was growing up I learned that my grandmother had had a nervous breakdown. No one in the family ever talked about it and my mother would change the subject whenever I asked, so it made me scared. The empty space had the same effect, like a vague, dark cloud casting a shadow over a corner of my soul. It made me feel anxious.

After a while Grandma's experience began to have an eroding effect on my confidence. I knew that I was living with a secret that I couldn't, or wouldn't, share. As a result, I felt alienated from my peers, from my neighbors, from my friends and especially my family. It's almost unbelievable to me now to think how angry I was with my parents because they were so out of touch with what I was going through. No one understood, though now I see that it was as much my fault because I kept it all in.

You know what I mean, don't you? You'd do the same thing. Anyone would after the strange looks I was getting when I tried to talk about it. I did try to talk about it at first and my mother got worried for me. My sister Lisa was mad at me for getting my mother all upset. I can see now that she was trying to protect her, but what about me? No one seemed concerned about what I was going through.

When my mother died that following spring my sister laid blame at my doorstep. She says mother thought I was going crazy and just couldn't deal with the notion of having her son committed to an asylum. Lisa says mother stopped eating one day and in the nursing home kept pulling the feeding tubes out. After the funeral my sister moved to California. She said she needed to get away from her crazy family and make a new beginning. I haven't seen or heard from her since.

The day my lease was fulfilled I found an apartment in St. Paul where I took on my first caretaker job. I've always been a handyman. That's where I met Linda, a student at Hamline University, who later became my wife. It bothers me though that in the seven years we've been married I never once mentioned the apartment with the empty space. She knows everything else about me, but I'm still afraid to tell her. If she didn't believe me, I don't know what I'd do. Isn't it ironic? I'm afraid the empty space will put a wall between us, so I keep it to myself. The result is a secret I feel I can't share, and so it separates us.

Should I say something, or bury it? I knew if you believed my story I'd feel hopeful that maybe she'll believe it, too. You do believe me, don't you?

Duel of the Poets

"Each year new consuls and proconsuls are made; but not every year is a king or poet born." Lucius Annaeus Florus c. 125

There is a little known principle - a secret law of the universe, as it were - that where two identical things simultaneously come into existence, one of them must cease to be, for there can be no two things exactly alike. This principle, like many spiritual laws, has been lost to our rational, mechanistic minds, though ancient philosophers and alchemists were aware of it and respected its power.

Borges made reference to this principle in his Personal Anthology, page 88, and it is a central feature of the story I am about to relate which was partially recorded in the History of Ammianus Marcellunus of the fourth century A.D.

The event took place during the reign of Marcus Tranquillius, an emperor known chiefly for his love of flowers, which has led some scholars to infer that he was more Greek than Roman. The fairest flower of the empire was a Court Poet of many years named Insepticus, whose name was being acclaimed throughout the Civilized World. As is not uncommon among poets Insepticus had, as a result of achievements, come to believe himself of greater significance than the empire itself. At a certain point in time he made a public pronouncement that he was unquestionably the supreme poet of his generation, if not for all time, and that undoubtedly the angels themselves were jealous of his glory.

Hardly a week had passed before there appeared at the palace gate a young poet from abroad who claimed that the gods, in a dream, had presented him with the gift of a poem which he was to deliver in the presence of Marcus Tranquillius. He asserted that he himself had been the Court Poet for a minor sheik in the kingdom of Kalenda Parnhu in the East. When word of the young poet's arrival reached the Emperor, the small hairs on his neck stood on end and his spine tingled, which gave him the impression that an affair of no small significance was on the verge of occurring.

An envoy was sent to retrieve the young poet. After three days of ceremonial cleansing and ritual instruction as regards behavior in the presence of a Roman Emperor, the young man was ushered into the Royal Court.

The sight of Insepticus, seated at the right hand of Marcus Tranquillius, impressed the young poet far more than the regal splendor of the court itself. Where else in the world could a mere poet attain to such honor?

After an evening of soporific speeches by unknown statesmen, Marcus Tranquillius at last stood to announce that the following morning there would be a Duel of the Poets with the entire assembly invited to attend to bear witness. Believing himself a spokesman for the gods, as is the custom of Emporers, Tranquillius assigned added gravity to the occasion by declaring, "The Deity Himself has ordained it," which, in fact, He had.

Throughout the evening Insepticus remained cool and composed, offering no indication that he was in any way intimidated by the young poet. Some later said that he did not sleep from the moment of the young poet's arrival, but these were only rumors and have no bearing on what actually occurred, as will soon become apparent.

The morning sun emblazoned the sky with symbolic significance as courtiers prepared the poets for this epic confrontation. Tranquillius, it is said, woke three hours before dawn, his heart leaping from excitement. No one knows what the young poet felt through that fateful night. It is known only that he had come to satisfy a perceived obligation.

The amphitheater had nearly filled by the time Tranquillius was seated. A signal was given and a hush permeated the crowds as the two poets were ushered to the great stage.

Insepticus, who needed no introduction, was to be the first to deliver. As had been agreed, each would take turns presenting portions of oratory for as long as was deemed necessary until either one or the other conceded.

Insepticus stepped forward and a great stillness ensued. At a decisive moment he opened his mouth, delivering with prosaic eloquence a self-portrait in sixteen quatrains.

It would appear that the poem had made an impression on the young poet, for a remarkable blaze appeared in his eyes, though none could comprehend its meaning. When the young poet moved forward, the elder stepped aside, but did not retire to the rear of the stage. He was evidently eager to see what topic this unproven wayfarer had selected. To his amazement, the young poet began to repeat, verbatim, and with even greater eloquence, the same exact words he himself had only moments before delivered, in sixteen quatrains.

Insepticus took a rather long moment to compose himself. He then delivered forty-four couplets on the same theme he had previously introduced, only in greater detail.

To the astonishment of all, the young poet, looking confident, repeated the forty-four couplets with great enthusiasm.

An imperceptible numbness seemed to seize upon Insepticus' brain. It was with great difficulty that he delivered his next sequence of stanzas which illuminated whole territories of his soul with remarkable exactitude.

The young poet continued his mimicry, only when it came to a certain particular in the twenty seventh stanza, the young poet diverged briefly to interject several additional particulars which Insepticus had omitted.

Upon completion of this specific sequence of stanzas by the young poet, Insepticus appeared to have regained a measure of his strength. Perhaps he feared that the duplication of his epic poem would eradicate it. The deviation which occurred in the twenty seventh stanza of the third section would suffice to deflate this fear. His next three segments were delivered with the fluency and ease that had brought him the accolades he knew himself worthy of and for which he had been appointed Court Poet.

The young poet, however, proved equally eloquent, and a sense of dreamlike unreality began to overcome the crowd.

It was early afternoon when the young poet again deviated from the mimcry which had heretofore prevailed in his oration. Insepticus had, in the fourth stanza of his sixteenth segment, hinted at a private struggle which perpetually shamed him, but was an essential ingredient in his greatness. The young poet broke off into a twenty eight measure chant revealing intensely intimate details of this struggle. Insepticus appeared crestfallen.

But it was a measure of his greatness that when his turn again came to speak, he picked up the thread of his rhetoric with the forcefulness and expressiveness that two decades of audiences had delighted in. For the subject was himself, and upon this theme he could elaborate with great zeal.

As the performance continued late into the afternoon, the portrait of Insepticus, as drawn by his own words, seemed flawless and wonderful, though in a few small details incomplete. However, it was precisely at these points of incompleteness that the young poet had brought the added measure of meticulous precision needed to fill out the picture. And when the young poet stepped forward for what would become the final segment of their performance, a strange look came upon him. For the tongue carries both a song and a sword. It has a magical power of which we are often most ignorant. And the young poet, who knew not the fullness of this power, felt himself filled with it, and frightened by it, though his fear did not refrain him from yielding to it.

And the portrait which was spoken, with its longings and renunciations, self-acceptance and self-reproach, dreams and denials, its manifold loves and bitter failings, this portrait of Insepticus was indeed so precise, so accurate that it did in fact succeed in being a duplication of the man himself. And when the young poet ceased from speaking, in the self-same instant the elder poet, Insepticus, the Court Poet of Marcus Tranquillius, disappeared. Vanished into ether.

The effect was hypnotic. Eyewitnesses could never agree exactly how it occurred. An awkward emptiness filled the city from that day onward.

As was anticipated, the young poet was afterwards appointed to the highest seat of honor in the kingdom; however, in the short period during which he held this office Marcus Tranquillius seldom appreciated the few mediocre poems he produced.

The young poet, whose modest output proved to be of a remarkably inferior caliber with little or no lasting merit, was in the end forced to resign, eventually returning to Kalenda Parnu in the East where his name has been forgotten to this day.

Lu Lee & the Magic Cat

"To live into the future means to leap into the unknown."
Rollo May

Once upon a time there was a lonely man named Lu Lee. He was a poor man. He lived in a small one-room house by himself, and he was often sad because he had no friends. He had no friends because he was different from other people and he lived in a land where people who are different are often made to feel unwelcome.

One day, as Lu Lee lay dreaming on his bed, he was visited by a Siamese cat, the most beautiful Siamese he had ever seen. The cat had come in through an open window and leaped up onto the bed with him.

As he stroked her silky cinnamon fur, she purred deeply so that Lu Lee closed his eyes and began to dream. He dreamed about the many girls he had loved from afar, and the many ways his heart had been broken because in the end he was different from others and he lived in a country where people who are different are made to feel unwelcome.

When he opened his eyes, he couldn't believe what he saw. A beautiful Oriental girl curled beside him, wrapped in a white towel, his hand gently gliding over the silkiness of her bare shoulder.

"Now this is a very beautiful dream," Lu Lee thought to himself, and he closed his eyes once more as she nestled beside him.

When he opened his eyes again, his hand was stroking the soft fur of the cat, whose dark eyes glistened brightly as she purred.

"Would you like some milk little kitten?" Lu Lee asked. The cat stood and stretched and seemed to nod.

Lu Lee found a container of milk and a bowl and brought them to the cat. In his excitement, he spilled some of the milk onto the floor.

"Do you have a name?" he asked as the cat lapped up the spilt milk. Then he said, "I'm going to call you Cinnamon." He said this because her silk fur was cinnamon colored, except for her black face.

After that, Cinnamon became Lu Lee's very special friend. For a whole summer, she visited him every single day.

But then one day, Cinnamon failed to appear at his window as she always had each morning leaving Lu Lee's heart broken anew.

"How can it be," Lu Lee said to himself, "that I have so loved this cat who brings me dreams? I am so lonely I could die. If only I were rich, I could buy gifts and I would have many friends. But I have nothing to give. I am just a poor man with nothing."

For many months he did not see the Siamese cat whom he had named Cinnamon. And while he longed with all his heart to see her again, he knew that cats have a mind of their own and must be left free to come and go as they please. It was a lonely, cold winter for Lu Lee, yet he comforted himself by remembering the magic dreams she had given him.

To Lu Lee's great surprise, when spring came the magical cat returned. He wasn't thinking of her at all when, suddenly, there she was standing silently on his window-sill. She looked different to him somehow. Tears of joy moistened his eyes. But there was a different look in Cinnamon's eyes this day. When he stroked her fur, she purred differently than before and when she became the beautiful woman of his dreams, she looked different, too, because she was now heavy with child, her tummy round and full.

Lu Lee said, "What's this?" He was quite astonished.

"This is your child, Lu Lee."

"But how can it be? You are only a dream," he replied.

"Ah, but not really. This is a magic dream, Lu Lee, and I am as real as you are. And so are your children."

"My children!" Lu Lee cried out.

"You will have many children," said the girl.

"But how can that be?" asked Lu Lee.

"You will see." And with these words she became a Siamese cat once more, only this time Lu Lee could see she was quite pregnant.

For half a morning Lu Lee watched the cat as she paced about the room, sticking her nose into every conceivable corner and cranny. At last, she sprawled out upon a thin, frayed cushion and patiently gave birth to seven tiny kittens. Lu Lee leaned over to watch as she nursed her wriggling, mewing kits, his eyes aglow with amazement and awe.

For several weeks Cinnamon stayed with Lu Lee, nursing her litter, until one night when he returned from a walk the cat was gone, leaving Lu Lee to take care of her seven babies. All that night he lay awake thinking what he should do. He even asked God what he should do, because he did not know what to do.

Now Lu Lee had an old overcoat with big pockets, and when the sun came up he took the seven kittens and placed them in the great pockets of his coat. He had determined that day to find homes for these kittens. He decided he would find seven children who had no fathers and present each with the gift of a kitten. In this way, he believed he should bring a moment of happiness to seven lives in the same way that his magic friend Cinnamon had brought a moment of happiness to his own lonely life.

As he walked through the town, he was surprised by how many lonely children he found. He knew the world was full of fatherless children, but how many he had no idea! As he began giving away his kittens, he soon realized that there were more children than gifts, and he almost began to be sad.

Then a strange thing happened. As Lu Lee was pulling the last kitten from his pocket, he felt something wriggle in his other pocket. "That's funny," he thought, for he was sure he had given away seven kittens. When another small boy with large dark eyes came up to him, he shared a kitten with this boy, too. And as he turned, he felt still more wriggling and felt down inside the pocket to discover yet another lively little furball. For that whole day, his pockets yielded an endless supply of kittens.

Word quickly spread of the miracle of the kittens and of Lu Lee's generosity.

The next day many of the children came to see him, to thank him. (Of course, a few came only to see more miracles or to see what else he might give them, because some people always like to get something for nothing.)

To each one that came, Lu Lee gave a story or a riddle or a game or told a joke. And it seemed there was no end to the stories, riddles and games, and no matter how often the children came, his imagination produced as much good cheer as his pockets had previously yielded kittens.

Lu Lee's happiness was great because he recognized that this was what the magical Cinnamon had meant when she said he would have many children.

In time, Lu Lee became the happiest man in all that country, for all the children who knew him loved him. And he loved them as well. He envisioned himself as father of them all.

When he was very old and full of years, it was said that Lu Lee had thousands of children, for the town had grown to be a big city that over time produced multitudes of children who had no fathers. Nevertheless, Lu Lee managed to find nearly every one, and to each he had given something special that could never be taken.

A few of us were with him the day he left this world for the next. To the end he lived simply in his modest one room house. He had often encouraged us to be dreamers and even on this last day he told us to hold onto our dreams. Yet it wasn't until the last pulses of sunset were being massaged into the horizon that he shared with us the secret of his joy. The room had become so still you could hear the petals closing on the tulips that lined his bedstead, and as day finally yielded to night, Lu Lee whispered, "There is no greater joy than giving." Smiling, he breathed his last.

Unrecorded Histories

Introduction to "An Unremembered History of the World"

There are some who have proposed that it is sheer vanity for us to imagine our earth as the only heavenly body populated by creatures with intelligence and personality. I propose that it is equally vain to imagine that our history, the one recorded by our historians, the one we know as "recorded history," is the only valid history for mankind here on this earth.

To imagine life on other galaxies and to search for it are not unrelated. As is well known, steps have already been undertaken to find evidence in support of this hypothesis.

In regards to the latter notion, that there exists the possibility of an infinite series of parallel times... verification of this theory is a task whose path is less self-evident, obscured as it is by mists. And yet, we see glimpses of it, reflected here and there from the great minds who were not bound to earth by the pettiness that so smothers us. Goethe noted that his heart contained the capacity for all acts, from the most heinous to the sublime. Could he have been standing on the threshold of those infinite courses that sweep into other avenues of time, unseen, unknown and unremembered?

Bernard Yachtmann records instances where people have had glimpses of other histories, reiterating the conviction that time contains an infinite number of parallel streams, and in each there are alternative histories, of an infinite variety. While not every act leads to significant consequence, many acts do, and what if, in an alternate history, the consequences of those acts were indeed being played out. Likewise one can find similar references by Marconi, Hasjammer, and Brandt, and an exhaustive treatise along these lines by Don Luis de Nativo.

While at the University of Salamanca at the turn of the century, Don Luis de Nativo wrote extensively on this theme. Though his manuscripts remained mostly unpublished and were eventually lost, the man de Nativo is best remembered as an archetype of de Unamuno's "man of passion" as fleshed out in *The Tragic Sense of Life*, de Unamuno's master work. (I have been told that it was a chance meeting with Joseph Conrad which prompted de Nativo to pseudonymously publish his epic work *El Mundo Gordo*.)

In other words, to get right to my point: my proposition is not original. It has been well documented by others as a reasonable conjecture. No doubt it is my own insecurity that forces me to cite other, more significant voices, as if the testimony of my own experience will be insufficient.

Those of you who know me know that I often have unusual dreams. Oftentimes the dreams unfold as detailed stories. I recently dreamt a short skit that became a television commercial. I've had prophetic dreams, including a dream that showed me my firstborn would be a son. I've also had dreams which I believe were gifts from God.

In September of 1984 I had a strange dream. As is my custom, I recorded the images of my dream, in as much detail possible, and its effect.

Two months later, while looking for a book by one author or another at one of our local used bookstores, I happened upon a small, Irish green, clothbound book called *Flight of Gypsies*. It was one of those moments when a small decision carries weight, when you feel compelled to act irrationally. The price, eight-fifty, was higher than I would have expected, especially considering the broken binding and what appeared to be several loose and missing pages. Yet when I opened the book and randomly read about five sentences, I knew that I must have the book.

I'd no sooner gotten the book home than I regretted the decision. The volume was more or less a compendium of prophecies by various gypsy seers in England, from 1632 to 1785. The purpose, I could only surmise, was to assemble a record of prophetic utterances for verification purposes. For the most part the sketchy accounts were repetitive and tedious and I soon found myself bored. There were prophecies about early deaths, unhappy marriages, deformed children, and blights on households to the third and fourth generations, utterances about flea infestations, curses of blindness and baldness, worms, contagion, and dementia. I put the book on a shelf in our garage.

The next day I found one of the pages lying on the floor next to my desk. With no intention of reading, I picked it up to deposit it in the trash when the name Thomas Olney caught my eye. Olney was the name of the man in my dream. To this man and his family I will need to return, in order to strengthen my arguments and make plain my case.

Not all dreams are stories, nor do all dreams reveal secrets about the nature of the universe -- though many reveal secrets about ourselves -- and I am often quite impressed with the power of this magic mirror of our souls.

Nevertheless, that night I began a quest, the result being this which you now read, of our unremembered history.... one of many, I might add... and one which we may all, with longing, seek to gain again.... if not for ourselves, then for our heirs.

An Unremembered History of the World

"I, Daniel, was deeply troubled by my thoughts, and my face turned pale, but I kept the matter to myself."

Daniel 7:28

1

When we speak of history, we must always remind ourselves that we are speaking only of "history as we know it." The task of historians to document, revise and debate the events and meanings of events in human history is a daunting one, even when simplified to contain only that which is known. (By known, I mean known by the human race in our specific line of experience from Adam to the present.)

We are not debating Adam and Eve here. That is a tedious debate that is ultimately a matter of faith. Rather, I am proposing that our historians make a greater effort to record the alternate histories, the streams that flow from alternate choices that could have been made throughout the courses of time.

In the village of Dunn on the outskirts of Devonshire, England, in the spring of 1698, a sequence of events occurred which would have a dramatic impact on the history of the world. Like the fabled grain of mustard seed, the events seemed small and would have otherwise gone unnoticed had they not been recorded in a journal that has been passed to us through the generations.

The thing that happened - or rather, the sequence of events that this story seeks to uncover beginning with this singular incident in the life of Thomas Olney, a Dunn tailor - is staggering to consider. Perhaps this is why our minds repress such knowledge. It is too weighty. But then, what if... Let us leave off from musings and examine that which we have come to know.

It is well known that in these parts nomadic tribes of gypsies passed with frequency and, on certain occasions especially associated with lunar convergences, the gypsies believed themselves to have the mystical ability to confer special powers to newborn infants.

Olney's wife had been in an unusually protracted labor. He feared her life was endangered. It was a particularly bitter blow to Olney, being naturally inclined to optimism as he was. The only town physician, his name is not important, had gone to the sea for a holiday. Because Olney had expected the good doctor to return in time to deliver the baby, he thus prevented his wife from going to stay with her sister in Devonshire where there were several doctors in service.

When it appeared that all was lost, that both mother and child would soon perish, Olney sent word to the gypsies to send someone who could help deliver his wife from her suffering. Three gypsy women arrived and his son was born within the hour. Partly out of gratitude and partly from delirium, the young father asked the gypsies to bless his son. The women wept and said it would be a privilege.

The boy, who was named Thomas after his father, was placed in the midst of a circle of candles. A strange ritual followed, with incantations in strange languages. The women rubbed a foul ointment on the infant's forehead and proceeded to prophecy. "One day, when this boy is a man, he will be permitted the gift of having one wish granted by the gods, when he wishes for it with all his heart. It will be like a dream, and the world will never be the same."

The prophecy was accompanied by a strange feeling of both elation and dread, which pierced Olney's heart like a thorn. He wondered what it would be that his son would wish for. And he wondered how the world would be changed.

Many years passed and as the boy grew the strange prophesy seemed to recede in importance. These were the days when England's disenfranchised had begun dreaming of a better life, a better hope, a better world across the seas... in America. A friend of young Tom Olney's had just returned from this new world and spoke in glowing images of a sprawling untamed land, luscious as Eden, {cf. J Warwick Montgomery, The Shaping of America, chap 1, Questing for a New Eden} where a man can put down his roots and truly be a man.

Olney's imagination was stirred. His parents knew it would only be a matter of time and their son would be swept away with the currents that drew dreamers to the American Colonies.

The day came more quickly than they supposed, however. A scandal broke out amongst the Brethren, the religious sect to which the Olneys subscribed, and young Tom was in the middle of it. In the spring of 1718, a certain Molly Hartwick, daughter of the venerable attorney Lyle Hartwick, was found to be with child. Though the proper thing was hurriedly carried out, there was no escaping the chatter that accompanied the newlyweds' every move about the village. By the time the child was born, Tom and Molly were so wearied by the galvanized glances and wagging tongues that they determined the only hope for a decent life for their young son was in the New World. Arrangements were made, farewells exchanged. They soon found themselves residents in a place called Berks County, Pennsylvania.

The transition to life on the American frontier was not terrifically difficult. There were many Quaker Brethren here, and the young family had hearts full of dreams. The land was good, the forests amply supplied with game. The increasing numbers of settlers were eager to help one another. Settlements of Delaware, Susquehannocks and Shawnee in that region had become accustomed to the presence of the white man and were no serious threat.

As an aside it should be remarked upon how fertile this new colony was to become in the shaping of future history. It is noteworthy that the forebears of Abraham Lincoln resided here, that the Daniel Boone legacy originated here, that

Benjamin Franklin and others of similar stature trace their roots to this selfsame soil. And most significantly, the firstborn son of Thomas Olney: Charles Rogers Olney

Two years later Molly gave birth to a robust redheaded daughter, Elizabeth Mary Olney. It was a difficult birth and afterward the Lord closed Molly's womb, leaving her unable to bear more children. Somehow they found this difficulty acceptable, and they rejoiced greatly in the two wonderful children that seemed to blossom under their care.

Over the course of years it seemed the Lord's hand of blessing was with this family in a special way. The fields Olney planted seemed to produce twice the harvest as his neighbors, and the skill, intelligence and character of the Olney children gained the Olney's recognition from as far away as Philadelphia. It was said that son Charles was fluent in four languages and on his fifteenth birthday demonstrated his mastery by reciting in four languages -- English, Dutch, French, and Shawnee, the local Indian tongue -- a short narrative he had written.

For all these blessings the elder Olney, with evident humility, gave all credit to our gracious and Almighty God.

Tragically, the tables turned and a series of devastating losses occurred, beginning with the death of the family dog which Olney's daughter found cruelly beheaded in a shallow stream near their home. The perpetrator of this horrible thing was a passing stranger who had been seen hanging around in town the previous week and who many believed to be demon possessed. The man disappeared and was never seen again, but the incident produced in Olney a great foreboding.

That fall heavy rains fell, lasting for several weeks, followed immediately by a severe cold snap. But for the potatoes, Olney's other crops rotted on the vines. Though publically he declaimed, "The Lord giveth, and the Lord taketh away," in his heart he began to be anxious, fearing still further losses.

It was February when the fire broke out that took his homestead and his wife. People say he was talking like a madman for days, blaming himself for the sin that led to his marrying Molly in the first place, though he loved her dearly and she him and that though God forgives He still punishes even though it doesn't seem right. It was the first that anyone had heard of the illegitimate conception.

Nevertheless, the church family pulled together to aid the wounded Olneys. The teenage children were housed with the Hamiltons while Olney himself was given a room with Robert Russell who promised not to leave his side till all was well. Olney wept bitterly and would not be comforted.

The gossip spread like an acid. In spite of the illogical nature of it, the neighbors began to wonder if Olney was not indeed cursed. He himself had said it, referring repeatedly to the brutal slaying of his dog as an omen. They were difficult days for everyone involved, as each searched his own heart and wondered the same. Even his best friends became awkward around him, and sensing this awkwardness, Olney knew inwardly that he was no longer at home here, that he had become an alien.

That spring the house was not rebuilt. Olney and his two children determined instead to move further west, to clear a new homestead, more isolated and remote, deeper in the Blue Mountains.

Of the difficulties that summer, the small crop, the ramshackle one room home--there is no need to create details that have so long been forgotten. What is known about this period is that people in those days experienced many hardships. In addition to disease and famine, the occasional Indian uprising presented a serious threat to personal safety .

For the sake of this story we are most concerned with an incident that took place during Shawnee uprising in the autumn of 1773.

2

The Olneys lived an isolated life under primitive conditions in a remote region of the Blue Mountains. They had not received news of the uprising, had no expectation of the event that changed not only the course of their own lives, but the courses of history as well.

Early that morning son Charles had gone off hunting for game as was his custom. Game was plentiful in those days and he needn't go far, but he was far enough off not to hear it when the Indian raid came. Charles was hunting toward the east and the small band of five Shawnee had stolen in from the west.

Old Tom (he appeared much older than he actually was) was seated on a wooden slat, lacing his boots, while Elizabeth washed carrots in a basin that passed for a sink. Suddenly two Indians burst into the cabin. Elizabeth screamed. Tom reached toward the place where he kept his rifle, but the gun had been left in the corner across the room and the first Indian went directly to it when he saw Tom's eyes snapping toward it.

Two more Shawnee cautiously entered the back entrance and the Olney's immediately became submissive. The Indians bound their wrists and ushered them off into the woods, heading west from where they had come.

When Charles returned to the cabin he swiftly discerned what had taken place. Before heading out to find his family, he studied the forest from inside the cabin. Figuring that he had been hunting to the east and not seen or heard anything, he decided to search the several paths headed west. But which direction had they gone? As he left the cabin he noticed on the ground a scar in the dirt that pointed northwest. It was a marker from his father, for Tom Olney, when he saw which direction the party was headed, pretended to stumble and as he attempted to rise he scratched the earth with the toe of his boot.

Charles crept cautiously through the old growth forest, wondering how long it would take and how much time lay between them. The Indians, however, were in a hurry to return to their tribe. The leader of the party had taken Tom's rifle and, from the way he handled it, appeared to know how to use it. The others, armed with tomahawks, arrows and bows, also shared the responsibility of carrying a bag of carrots and some clothing which they had taken from the Olney homestead.

After two hours of hard walking Elizabeth fell exhausted and the Indians allowed them all to rest. One of the natives departed to see if they were alone in the woods or being tracked. He returned to the group and said something which neither Tom nor Elizabeth could understand.

Charles found the trail easily. His father and sister had been discreetly breaking tips of branches to mark the way so that Charles could rescue them. Nevertheless, the tracking was tedious and several times the young man had lost his way and had to return to where he was confident and try another route.

The rest period was brief and the war party moved on, only more slowly now. They seemed in a better mood, talking and laughing for the first time that day.

As evening approached one of the natives shouted something and they all became very still. Tom could see that they were all quite young, the one no more than a boy, and he thought of his own son, wondering if he would ever see him again. At no time did the Indians speak to them in a language they could understand and Tom regretted that he had not learned the native tongues his son Charles had mastered. His inability to figure out their intentions created an increasing anxiety that shackled his thoughts.

The Indian with the rifle had a twisted mouth which gave him a grim appearance. He stood watching while the others gathered branches and brush to build a small campfire. Olney had been shoved to the ground near a tree and his ankles were tight bound with twine. He swiveled himself around in an attempt to get comfortably situated, but finally lay on his side facing what would soon become a campfire.

Olney's thoughts were torn. Part of him wished for his son to arrive and rescue them. The other part of him felt absolute horror at the thought of losing both of his children in one day. He recalled a fragment of scripture about the futility of life, that whether we have been good or evil, the same destiny awaits us all.

The whole thing happened so quickly it was incomprehensible. For Olney, it was as if he were watching a drama, the players at this point being the five Indians and his daughter. His daughter was standing to the left of his field of vision and the leader with the rifle no more than fifteen feet away directly before him, three other Indians in the background. The fifth Indian had come up behind the daughter and put his hand on her shoulder.

Instantly, he heard a loud shout behind him and knew it was Charles. "Noooooooooooooo!"

The Indian with the twisted mouth swung the rifle up to his shoulder and took aim. Olney went totally berserk, his eyes nearly busting out of his head. In the deepest part of his heart, with his soul and with his whole being he wished the Indian to disappear, to no longer be there....no, there was a prayer forming, and uttered it like a command: "Become a tree."

The rifle fell and when the butt hit the ground it fired up into the treetops. When the sound died away all was still. Everything seemed to stop and all of them, the four Indians and the three Olneys, remained entranced by what they had witnessed. Where the Indian with the rifle had been standing there now stood a small oak.

It seemed hours, but was perhaps only a minute, and the four Indians scattered into the woods. Olney himself was shaking his head back and forth, knowing that somehow in some way a deep magic had worked in him to create this wonder. A hushed silence pervaded the forest floor, and then gradually there were the birdsongs and a chippering of ground squirrels.

Charles cut his father free from his bindings and the three of them walked close to the oak.

"How did you do this?" Elizabeth asked.

"Why do you say I did this? God must have done this."

For a long time they held each other and cried, old Tom Olney crying more deeply than he imagined possible. "It's all right, Father," Charles said.

Olney took out a knife and gouged an X on the side of the tree. It seemed to him that one day he would perhaps need to find this place again and remember it. Turning to his children, "God has spared us for a purpose. Touch this tree here, and remember this day. God has spared you for a purpose."

After passing the night in the woods the Olneys returned home to their cabin.

"I want to go to Philadelphia," Charles said the next day and his father agreed that this would be good.

3

It happened that back east in Philadelphia young Charles made the acquaintance of a certain Mr. Trent who introduced him to a Mr. Benjamin Franklin. As apprentice and protege to Mr. Franklin, Charles' linguistic fluency and marked self-assurance enabled Olney to obtain entrance to the most influential persons of the age.

His unique ideas about Destiny resulted in a series of debates in Parliament with regard to the future of the Colonies. The combined effect of his writings and the distribution of his ideas via the presses of Franklin led to a Declaration of Freedom in 1775. Without the shedding of blood a Nation of Colonies was born called the United States of America.

Olney became an Ambassador to Europe and travelled extensively. His ideas regarding freedom, trust and Destiny had a broad impact there as well. On his second journey he brought with him sister Elizabeth who remained there and became a Countess in the region now called Austria. Her influence among the Courts of Europe inspired Napoleon to dismantle his armies and ushered in the first Hundred Years Peace.

Meanwhile, in the United States a certain Rogers Olney, first-born son of Charles, after touring the Southwest Territories determined that a Fairness Doctrine should be developed with regards to the treatment of lands yet divided. Rogers' vision for a Fruitful Self-Determination became the underpinning of a Mutual Respect Policy between the United States and Santa Ana, then reigning in Mexico. In one of the most remarkable agreements in history, a settlement was reached whereby the Southwest was provided the opportunity to freely determine its future direction. Ultimately, a half-century later, this became the Open Border Policy, with a free exchange of wealth and cultural enrichment flowing in both directions. The resultant stability south of the border provided a foundation for peaceful development in all of Latin America. From 1820 onward there were no more revolutions in Mexico and widespread freedom and advancement for all nations to our south.

In the late 1840's Harrison Olney had begun to see the importance of resolving the slavery issue in this country and undertook it as his life work. His cousin, the late Marshall Fleming, as an aide to Disraeli, had successfully ushered England to an emancipation for its slaves, without rancor, without cost of life.

Harrison, grandson of Charles, thrice brought his eloquent tongue to the Supreme Court, and to the United States Congress on several occasions. Due to his influence, an equitable emancipation was achieved in 1855, without bloodshed. The country continued to prosper.

With the rich natural resources of its land and the abundance of ingenuity, America rose swiftly to new heights in the world older, respected for its ethics, industriousness and compassion. Descendants of Charles and Elizabeth Olney became leaders in industrial, academic and political life. It came as no surprise that, in 1880, an Olney became 18th president of the United States.

The influence of Olneys in Europe was equally remarkable. More than a century had passed without a significant armed conflict. When factions threatened the stability of Europe in the early Twentieth Century, it was Sir William "Sparky" Donovan, great grandson of Countess Elizabeth, who calmed the waters and provided a safe passage for future generations.

In 1920's Germany, because of the economic boom and the lack of a catalyst, a young malcontent named Hitler failed to gain popular support for his strange notions of a Master Race. His fiery rhetoric found no home in the hearts of his hearers, and he resigned himself to operating a pub in

Munich where he spent his years developing novel and pointless theories of world conquest.

In Russia, Communism likewise failed to take hold. Affectionately known to the Royal Court as Sir Sparky, Donovan persuaded the Tsar to distance himself from the power-mad Rasputin. Once free of Rasputin's influence, a change came over the royal family and generosity became the ruling ethic of the new era. With its own vast natural resources and an open society, Russia likewise experienced economic growth that invited the united participation of its several regions.

In short, the achievements of the descendants of this one man, Thomas Olney, reverberated throughout the world. In fact, descendants of Olney gained distinction in every field of endeavor, from anthropology to zoology, linguistics to physics, literature and the arts to economics and finance.

In the late twentieth century, Judith Remington-Olney, a biologist and high ranking official in the Red Leaf Foundation (an organization devoted to studying the relationship between trees and humans) developed the notion that it is possible to communicate with trees, that every tree has a story and if one were properly attuned, these stories could contribute in some way to human understanding. (The impetus for her ideas came from a fragment of a dream in which a tree became a man and she heard a voice saying, "I see men as trees walking.")

Remington-Olney enjoyed hiking through the forests of Pennsylvania near where she lived in the Blue Mountains. Her father told her stories about the Olneys who settled in Pennsylvania a long time ago, and she often wondered what it must have been like so deep in the wilderness, so far from civilization. She wondered, too, if some of the trees in these old hills once knew her great great great great grandparents. And she often wondered what tales they would tell if they could speak. It was during these hikes that she cultivated her theories of Biological Communication.

What if trees really were the souls of men? What if the spirits of the dead were the Life Force that germinated the seeds of trees in the forest? What if Heaven was nothing more than becoming a tree, arms outstretched, in perfect harmony with the world, ever worshiping the life-giving sun?

These were strange thoughts, but stranger still was her conviction that she could, by some deep magic of the forest, turn a tree into a man. Where this notion came from, from God or the devil, she knew not. It was a powerful idea and it gripped her like nothing ever had before.

4

Judith Remington-Olney stretched out on her back beneath an enormous oak tree. She studied its wrinkled hide and asked it questions. Her eyes traced the knots and gnarls that make an old tree fascinating. She pondered the questions she might ask the tree, and it was then it happened. A reverberation in the earth had begun, so subtle that had she not been attuned to it, she would never have felt it. But there it was, and it made her fearful with excitement.

She, too, trembled and, standing, went near to the tree to feel its fractured and furrowed bark. As she put her arms around the trunk, her fingertips discovered and caressed the scarred X which had been carved into the tree's side twenty-five decades ago and she remembered a story which had been told to her in childhood about an Indian that had been turned into a tree. It was a fable, a tall tale, she had been led to believe. Her parents always said it was something like the stories of Paul Bunyan and Pecos Bill and all the rest of those early American mythologies that evolve with the frontier.

Now she wondered. These were the blue hills. Could this be the place?

She tried to remember how she had gotten here. One day she would return to this tree and unfold its power.

For two years she gathered together all the family stories, trying to understand her roots. She read with great interest the many books about Olneys in history. She was especially interested in their motivations. Why had her family gone so far in making a mark on the world? What event could have transformed a frontier family into one of the leading families of their time, in every time in which Olneys were found?

Judith Remington-Olney re-read the old diaries, and weighed the words carefully.

For another five years she researched the rituals and myths of every culture seeking any and all tales of transformation, and especially transformations pertaining to trees. And as she uncovered the buried histories of our earliest ancestors she found echoes in each of the tale of trees. Even the Holy of Holies in Yahweh's Temple was engraved with cherubim and trees. "I am like a green palm tree," the Psalmist wrote.

Like the story of the flood, which is repeated in a hundred different traditions, she found the image of the tree as a core image in nearly every culture.

But even still she was not satisfied. She must release the spirit in the tree. And for this, a deeper ritual would be needed. And so it was that beneath a stack of books at a library sale she unearthed that rare volume of prophecies called *Flight of Gypsies*.

Judith became dizzy and lightheaded when she found it. Though she handled it with care, the binding broke when she opened the book. The page before her was titled, "Spell For Turning Trees Into Men". The book nearly dropped from her hand.

In very large letters there had been printed a warning:

"History will revert to the moment the man became a tree. Beware: This is a Fifth Circle event."

5

At this point you must be wondering why someone would do such a thing? Why would someone play with the Circles of Time? Why would someone risk everything to gain nothing?

Perhaps she did not take seriously the warning. Perhaps she did not understand it. Perhaps she could not resist the temptation to "see what would happen if...." It was all too far-fetched. Certainly no human could have the power to turn back time. It was not conceivable.

So it was that Judith Remington-Olney reached beyond the sacred wall that separates men from gods and having found a hole in that wall she reached in, only to be bitten by the serpent waiting there. No sooner had the salve been applied to the base of the tree, the incantation uttered, the incense burned and the delirious ritual executed, an immense cascade of sound split the air.

The rifle blast hit the advancing Charles square in the chest, knocking him backward off his feet. Elizabeth shrieked. The Indian beside her struck her fiercely with his tomahawk, dropping her to the ground like a stone, her skull crushed in. Tom Olney's eyes rolled up into his head as he breathed his last prayer. "Oh God, let me die." It was swift and severe.

The future that he never knew, the peace and prosperity of Destiny's children had been undone in a single moment.

The Nonsense Room

"Greg, I don't want you going in there tonight."

"Oh?"

"I mean it. It's starting to--"

"It's making me different somehow?"

"I didn't say that."

"But you'd like to say that. The room is changing me and you don't like it, is that it?"

"I'm scared, Greg."

He put his arm over her shoulders. "There, there."

"It's just a room," he wanted to say, but he knew it was more than that. He had discovered a world, a strange world, and he was fascinated by it, wanted to understand what made it work.

"It's not just a room," she said.

"Did I say it was 'just a room'?" he replied, startled.

"You were thinking it."

As he turned away from her and stalked down the hall he had a thought, brief but vivid, that his relationship to this room would lead to a reckoning; but the thought slid away from him and escaped from his consciousness so that he was unable to retrieve it and could only hear in his mind the hollowness of the false comfort he offered while feigning paternalistic concern, saying, "There, there."

"Greg!" his wife cried as he twisted the handle to the Nonsense Room, but he disregarded her and went in. He was not interested in having his life constricted by his wife's fears and he was baffled by their intensity.

Eyes flaming, Leslie fell to the sofa and lit a cigarette.

For Greg and Leslie Moore, finding a home in Stillwater, Minnesota, was more problematic than originally imagined, but at the last they discovered the Shatterly Place, an enormous hodgepodge of competing architectural motifs ambitiously stapled together with Victorian pretensions. Marketed as a handyman's special, the price was most appealing. Only later did they learn of the strange history of the house. "People get deranged in that house," the grocer told Leslie at Thanksgiving. "The place either finds 'em cracked or leaves 'em that way."

The Nonsense Room wasn't discovered until the following spring. They were rearranging the kitchen and decided to move the old refrigerator out of an alcove that they planned to turn into a pantry. Behind the refrigerator they discovered a door with a hasp, padlocked shut. The door, hinges, hasp and lock had all been painted mint green, a reminder that the fifties had passed this way. The ceiling of the alcove was dingy with cobwebs, and greasy. The floor, too, was rank with grunge. But Greg saw only the door.

"Where do you think it goes?" Greg said.

Leslie reminded him of the rumors that circulated in town regarding the house.

Using a hammer and chisel, Greg mangled the hasp. As he turned the knob the motor kicked in on the fridge, giving them both a fright.

The room was little bigger than a closet, no more than four feet deep and perhaps six feet wide, the walls and ceiling completely overspread with pictographs, calligraphy, scribbles and assorted mystical inscriptions seemingly as countless as the stars.

"It gives me the creeps," Leslie said.

Greg found the writing on the walls intriguing, but he didn't say anything. After Leslie had gone to bed that night, Greg found a lantern that he could set on the floor to study the closet room in more detail.

For a long time he simply stood scanning, taking in the big picture, much as a man might take in the immensity of a night sky upon his first experience of it away from the bright lights of the city. His first impression, which he suppressed--reasoning that it was impossible--was that it was infinite, that the closet scribblings simply had no beginning and no end.

Even his initial cursory study of the closet's walls instilled in Greg a sense that there were relationships amongst the clusters of words and images. He was reminded of early cave men studying the night sky, noting and naming its constellations. Sections of the closet seemed to contain whole galaxies of graffiti.

What first caught his attention and attracted him to the room's details was a tiny pyramid on the far wall opposite the door at the top of which was drawn, with a fair amount of exactitude, an eye with lines radiating out from it. Greg was on his knees inside the closet studying the detail in the pupil of the eye. Upon closer inspection, he observed that the spokes which shot out from the eye were in actuality lines of fine print, much of it readable, some of it too minute or too poorly scrawled to decipher.

With both apprehension and wonder he became absorbed with reading bits and pieces of text, some of it hinting toward meanings, albeit obscure ones at best, but most of it elusive and cryptic. Thus he read,

"An esoteric religiosity of the Unconscious"

and

"Powers, the abyss, Numen and Tremendum"

and

"This is the God that the sense of the sacred feeds upon"

and

"This same God is often shown in an opposite way"

and

"Infatuated with the awesome and the fascinating"

and

"In speaking of Him we celebrate our ignorance."

There were also Latin and Hebrew texts, hieroglyphic symbols, and codified images that appeared to have some sort of ceremonial significance.

What happened after that began to disturb him. It was the pyramid with the eye which first captivated him, and he returned to his knees in order to find it, but could not, and it frustrated him. It had been a small icon for sure, but not so small as to be impossible to locate again, and he began systematically examining the region of the closet where he had first observed it, to no avail, and it set his nerves on edge so that the night's sleep which followed proved fitful and unsatisfying.

Before leaving for the bank the next morning (he worked as an auditor there) Greg resisted a strong urge to return to the closet room for "one more little peek." This did not relieve him of its influence, however, as he spent much of his day distracted by the effects he experienced in the closet the night before.

"Honey, I'm home," he shouted that evening upon coming in the door. Hearing no greeting in reply he tensed up and walked hastily to the kitchen. "Leslie?" he called again. He hurried to the closet room and was opening it just as his wife entered the kitchen from the yard.

"Is something wrong?" she said.

"I, well, you didn't answer when I came in. I just-"

"What would I be doing in that stupid old closet?" She recognized by the uneasy fear that revealed itself in his face that the closet had made an impression upon him as something dangerous, something to be reckoned with. This realization made her uncomfortable.

All through supper he was absent from her, waiting to be finished with the task of eating. What he found dreadful was the role-playing, pretending nonchalance about both what had happened and about his plans for the evening. When the dishes were washed he proceeded to the closet room. She said nothing to dissuade him.

He set about directly to locate the original eye symbol but his determination was only half hearted. Instead, playing explorer-philosopher Greg began reading again the varied and unusual collage of inscriptions, at first casually, and then with a growing desire to comprehend.

Unfortunately, the sentences fluctuated between legibility and illegibility, leaving him with only partial meanings and suggested texts. Nothing was complete, nothing wholly cohesive.

Nightly, for more than seven weeks, Greg gave himself to the closet, an activity that left him both stimulated and disturbed. Never once in that time did he find again a phrase, symbol or inscription which he had previously encountered. This proved to be a frustration only when he allowed himself to become obsessed with seeking such a thing.

What frustrated him more was that the meanings of the texts almost seemed to make sense, perpetually holding out the promise that a measure of persistence would yield a treasure of understanding. But there was no reward. No treasures of understanding were grasped.

From time to time he stepped back to take in the whole. He looked for and sometimes found constellations or clusters of word groupings, but like the initial image that had captured him in the beginning the relationships he recognized so clearly only moments before seemed to have receded from view and became impossible to locate again.

There was a common mystical quality to the inscriptions he read. Phrases such as, "There is not a more crucial notion of force"

and

"determinism, theism and some brands of physics"

and

"it is God alone who coordinates created effects"

and

"towards which the human feels at once attraction" seemed to suggest something of a cosmology here.

The phrases at first appeared arbitrary and unrelated, other than the common thread of metaphysical suggestiveness. This last phrase invigorated him because he saw that the word "attraction" must be followed by the words "and repulsion." The sudden insight made him dizzy. It was as if he had come into close proximity with something so extraordinary he was incapable of apprehending it.

Upon reflection later he might have said it was as if his consciousness, his inner ability to comprehend meanings, were somehow like a series of out of focus lenses which, if brought into harmony, would provide a clarity of inner vision like nothing he could have ever imagined. It seemed as if the shifting of these lenses into synchronicity was accompanied by a tingling sensation inside his skull and--here he couldn't be sure for it was so vague and foreign an experience he didn't know what to make of it--some kind of aural musical accompaniment not unlike wind chimes and pan pipes. Something deep inside him--from his soul? from his subconscious?--was being awakened, and this awakening was accompanied by both anticipation and an uncanny foreboding.

Their last meal together began with a long silence. Leslie had determined not to speak until Greg made notice of her muteness. When she finally caved in, she was incapable of concealing her exasperation.

"Don't you remember what day this is?" Her eyes avoided his for fear of his answer. He stopped chewing but made no reply.

"Greg, talk to me. What's happened to us? I don't even know you any more."

He looked down at the floor. "It goes both ways. There are things I'd like to talk about with you, too, but I know you don't want to hear it."

She didn't reply, staring now at a spot on the table.

"I'm not Mister Wonderful. But I'm not the only one shutting people out. Look, I'm sorry I forgot our anniversary. Will you forgive me?"

"That's not what this is about," she said sharply, tears brimming in her eyes.

He pushed his chair away from the table, stood and walked haltingly to the sink, trying to read her with small, discreet glances.

"You're not going in there again tonight. Not tonight." It wasn't quite a question; she was pleading. She stood up, half uncertain as to what she should do, whether to rush and cling to him or to flee.

He nodded as if considering her words, noisily scraping his plate and rinsing it.

"Why don't I run to town and get a video. Is there anything in particular you've been wanting to see?" He turned away from her and walked from the kitchen without looking back.

"Damn you, Greg."

As Leslie pulled from a drawer the unopened card that she had planned to give him she marked it as the first time she had allowed herself to consider that she had made a mistake in marrying this man. The argument with which she normally consoled herself--We've had our difficulties, but who hasn't?--temporarily yielded and would not support her. She steadied herself with both hands against the counter, tears streaming over flushed cheeks.

With the clack of the latch she knew him to be gone from her forever. She stared at the empty kitchen as if seeing for the first time. She hated this place now. Into the hall, to the living room, to the bedroom--Leslie stumbled from room to room without aim, the internal fever of emotions draining her of strength, until she found herself slumped in the corner of the couch near the window. Hands trembling, she lit a Virginia Slim, took a couple strong pulls and lay the cigarette on a red ceramic trivet on the armrest of the couch.

"Greg?" she called. "I'm going for a walk. Will you come with me?" "Greg!" she cried sharply, now standing.

Leslie staggered from the house to the unfettered freedom of an open sky. Inside, a burst of air from the window rolled the still-lit cigarette off the trivet so that it fell between the cushion and the arm.

There were few houses along this section of bluff overlooking the river, which had been a large part of its appeal when they chose to move here. A string of summer cabins, unoccupied this time of the year, dotted the woods where the road dipped down to the river's edge, but the bluff itself had been long ago cleared for horse grazing and McAllen's sod operation. She walked slowly, not looking back. Upon reaching the perimeter of the sod farm she took a familiar path through the trees that meandered lazily down the hillside toward the river below. The usual pestering by mosquitoes was kept at bay by the breezy evening air. As the shadows of evening descended she stopped to lean against a tree for support, pestered instead by a swarm of anxious thoughts. One of these broke through as she remembered the Slim on the arm of the couch. She turned and headed back up the hillside through the trees.

When she saw the angry pulsing glow of firelight through the windows of her house, she gasped, both stunned and alarmed.

Leslie made a hasty decision to dart across the road to the nearer McAllen's rather than directly back home, needing desperately to alert the fire department. She could see a light on and prayed someone was at home. Leslie banged on the front door. No answer. She tried the handle and, finding it locked, despairingly crashed her fists against the door. She scrambled to the side of the house, found the kitchen door open, burst in, and called 9-1-1.

Dashing from the house, she began trotting toward home as fast as she dared, knowing a sprint would leave her winded before reaching her yard. Suddenly she stopped, whirled about and raced to the McAllen's house once more. She picked up the phone, dialing her own number this time, her breathing hoarse and laborious.

Answer the phone, Greg. Answer the phone. Dear God, Greg, answer the phone.

Inside the nonsense room Greg had begun entering a new dimension of illumination, having placed himself once more under the influence of the room's spell, gradually having no awareness apart from it, no reality apart from the strange and cryptic reality of those four walls. His breathing was steady and deep as he entered the trance, knowing the meaning of trance, knowing what a trance is, feeling it and knowing it and how it gets deeper and releasing himself deeply into it; he began to have feelings of nostalgia as if somehow he were being awakened to a lost childhood. And still... further back, within himself... he sees... feels....

A palpable tension was followed by shortness of breath and expectation. At a certain point, a reversal took place and he made a profound connection between the images on the wall and the images in his mind. Not the first time he made this connection, but in previous trances he had interjected rational explanations, telling himself that these were nothing more than afterimages on the retina of his eyes. On this night he short-circuited the rationalizations, turned away from them and denied them their power.

From somewhere deep inside himself the music welled up again, beginning with wind chimes and pan pipes, music which he had previously named the Song of the Earth. And it was very beautiful and he knew he was part of something bigger than himself, something he wanted badly to be part of, and he couldn't understand why there were so many barriers in life, why everything had always been so difficult to comprehend. In the Song of the Earth he was able to lose himself, to escape all the questionings which wrapped about his mind like tentacles, to swim free in the milky waters of that earlier time, before he knew words, before he knew confusion, that age of ignorance and innocence which now appeared to be within his grasp.

The Song became loud and mighty and with his voice--haltingly at first, then with enthusiasm--he joined the boisterous throng. It seemed he had never felt so happy, and when the telephone rang, it was all part of the symphony of sound which had been swelling up within him, caressing him with sensations of heat and warmth, invigorating him with flashings of light from the dome of his imagination.

For some strange reason he had an overwhelming desire to remove his clothing, a desire which he refused to question or resist so that when his body was found, he was discovered naked, lying on his back with his head awkwardly wedged into the corner of the small room.

The fire was mentioned in articles that appeared in both the St. Paul and Minneapolis newspapers as well as the Stillwater Gazette, but with few details. While the circumstances surrounding Greg's death brought a measure of speculation regarding the issue of foul play, news reports indicated that as yet there were no charges pressed. The statements Leslie made implying that she deliberately set the fire were dismissed and attributed to her initial hysteria.

For weeks Leslie alternately blamed and excused herself, knowing that she had truly wanted to destroy him, yet knowing also she once loved him deeply and would miss him always. She did not yet know that for years to come she would become fearful in the presence of any hostile thought or emotion which she bore toward another.

One evening shortly thereafter, in the motel room where she had taken temporary refuge, she found a strange book which had been tucked in a drawer of the end-table where Gideon's Bibles are frequently found. As she thumbed through the book--obliquely titled *The Secrets of Experience*-- an inscription on one of the pages captured her attention. It was a tiny pyramid, at the top of which was drawn an eye with lines of text radiating from it.

The image unsettled her and she closed the book. However, a curiosity about the image would not leave her. Later, she attempted to again find the image, to study it further in order to learn its meaning. Being unable to find it left her greatly disturbed.

Acknowledgements

Those who have helped and encouraged me over the years are too numerous to name. I will, however, mention Portuguese artist Margarida Sardinha whom I interviewed for my Ennyman's Territory blog this past winter. Upon reading my stories she nearly insisted that I make an effort to get them published so they could be shared with a wider audience. This volume is a first step in that direction.

I would be remiss not to mention John Prin, my first mentor who demonstrated the importance of aiming high and not compromising when it came to the execution of one's vision. Thank you, John, for your example and three decades of encouragement.

Special thanks to TJ Lind, co-founder of N&L Publishing, who helped make this book possible and to Andrew Perfetti for designing its cover.

Ed Newman

Pioneerproductions.blogspot.com

Made in the USA
Monee, IL
29 December 2023